Sallie F Toler

Bird's Island

A Drama in Four Acts

Sallie F Toler

Bird's Island
A Drama in Four Acts

ISBN/EAN: 9783741187575

Manufactured in Europe, USA, Canada, Australia, Japa

Cover: Foto ©Andreas Hilbeck / pixelio.de

Manufactured and distributed by brebook publishing software
(www.brebook.com)

Sallie F Toler

Bird's Island

BIRD'S ISLAND

A DRAMA IN FOUR ACTS

BY

MRS. SALLIE F. TOLER

AUTHOR OF "HANDICAPPED," ETC., ETC.

CAST OF CHARACTERS.

ALFRED RAYBURN—Owner of Bird's Island.
DR. FONTAINE—His physician.
RICHARD SELWYN—His friend.
ARTHUR POWERS—An Englishman.
LARRY FISH—An Irishman.
STELLA RAYBURN—A little savage.
MADAM HELGA—Bertha Rayburn.
MRS. MCKILLOP—From a famous old Scotch family.
BOBBINETTE—A Creole servant.

FONTAINE and SELWYN, may be played by one gentleman.

Plays, two and one-half hours.

COSTUMES.

Rayburn, Selwyn and **Fontaine** wear ordinary suits of to-day. **Powers'** clothes should be after the broadest and latest English styles. **Larry** can wear large checks and flashy necktie.

Stella's first costume is a yellow satin short dress, trimmed in black lace and sequins. She wears a plain travelling-dress later in the first act. Second and third acts girlish house-dresses of good material. **Madam Helga** wears a street-costume at first entrance, other costumes light house-dresses. Wears gray hair and glasses.

Bobbinette should be dark and her dress should show many bright colors. Large hoop earrings should be worn throughout. Roberta, costumes, house-dresses well made. **Mrs. McKillop,** severe and prim dresses and manner of dressing her hair.

BIRD'S ISLAND.

ACT I.

[Scene : *Exterior of* **Rayburn's** *house at Bird's Island. The bay in the distance, with beach and landing for boats, in the foreground hammocks are swung, and tropical plants about. A Florida coast.* **Rayburn** *and* **Dr. Fontaine** *discovered at rise of curtain.*]

Dr. F. I tell you, Rayburn, it is inevitable, you mʏ ˙ realize it yourself ; you are growing worse every day.

Ray. It is too true, God help me, I am growing blind. Blind. I am blind already ; I can no longer see my daughter's face, Fontaine, only an indistinct blur when she stands before me.

Dr. F. How have you kept it from her so long ? She is unusually quick of perception, too. You are determined then to send her away from you ? Is this sacrifice necessary ? You will miss her, old friend.

Ray. [*Rising and pacing the walk.*] I will not sacrifice her young life to a selfish wish of mine. I will send Stella to New York to my old friend Richard Selwyn, Richard is one of the few men whom I have found true ; peculiar, but staunch as steel.

Dr. F. You abandon your plan then, of bringing up your daughter away from the conventialisms of society ? The free untrameled spirit we had hoped to make of her ?

Ray. I must ; hard as it is for me to part with her, I can not keep the truth from her much longer, and I am not strong enough to bear her grief, nor weak enough to blight her youth with my wretchedness.

Dr. F. But she must learn of your blindness some day.

Ray. Perhaps, after she has become familiar with other things and people, but I fancy I shan't live long, Fontaine.

5

Dr. F. Nonsense, man, your infirmity makes you morbid.

Ray. But you say yourself that my heart is weak.

Dr. F. Stuff. Only a slight functional disorder ; your heart is well enough. You'll outlive me yet. When does she go ? Have you told her yet ?

Ray. I have not told her, but she goes to-day.

Dr. F. To-day !

Ray. At four o'clock to-day, Andrew takes her to the mainland. Bobbinette goes with her, and the captain of the " Neptune " meets them. They go by steamer, and Selwyn is to meet them in New York.

Dr. F. To-day, and you have not told her. Rayburn, I had not thought you such a coward.

Ray. Ah, my dear friend you have never had an only daughter.

Dr. F. No, no, thank heaven ; not that only daughters are not very well as other people's daughters, but the suddenness of it all.

Ray. Better have one wrench of it than a lingering unhappiness for both of us.

Dr. F. Perhaps you are right. [*Rising.*] Well, I must be off for the mainland, or my patients will become impatients. I wish I could say something to comfort you, Rayburn. It is— the whole thing is an entirely uncalled for immolation of yourself. Why should you be buried here ? Why not go to New York yourself, and live surrounded with the comforts and friends which your wealth could bring you.

Ray. I will never leave this island.

Dr F. Oh, well, I suppose you know your own affairs best ; but I say it is a senseless sacrifice. I suppose now, you have no idea where the child's mother is ?

Ray. No, somewhere in Europe. But I cannot speak of her.

Dr. F. Is there any possible chance, Rayburn, that you may have been mistaken about her guilt ? Forgive me, but you know your unfortunate temper, and your equally unfortunate firmness.

Ray. [*Crossing to* L.] Why do you probe my soul with these questions ? I tell you I saw the woman whom I called my wife, with her lover at her feet ; saw him take her in his arms, while she clung weeping to his neck. The scene is graven on my brain, I think my eyes swim in a sea of blood at the sight. This blindness, Fontaine, is red like that. God ! How can you torture me with the memory of it ?

Dr. F. Forgive me, old friend, I will not offend again. You are sorely tried, and good-bye, Rayburn, I see Andrew out there with the boat. [*Ex. at landing.*]

Ray. How much bitterness can a man bear, how much sorrow endure, and yet live. My wife, the only woman I ever loved, and whom I believed as pure as an angel from heaven, false as she was fair ; and now, I must give up my one treasure, my little Stella. Blind ! Ah, my God—blind. It is too much. Never to see my darling's face again ! Never to watch the grace of growth as she advances toward womanhood. Blind ! [*Ex.* **Stella's** *voice is heard outside, laughing and talking. Music for Spanish dance. Enter* **Stella** *and* **Bobbinette.**]

Stella. Come on, come on ; dance it again, do, Bobbinette.

Robbi. Oh, oh—but young mistress. I am—too—too—old —fat, I'm out of breath. It is too violent.

Stella. Why, Bobbinette, what a story. You old ! you are only lazy, and not so very fat. Well then watch me and see if I do it right. [*Dances one or two measures.*]

Bobbi. Excellent, good. But I feel not in the humor for dancing to-day.

Stella. Now you've been dreaming again, Bobbinette.

Bobbi. 'Tis true, young mistress, and a bad omen too.

Stella. Foolish Bobbinette. What is it ?

Bobbi. [*Reading from a dream book taken from her pocket.*] "To dream of cabbage boiling in the pot, denotes ill luck, unless the pot be of glass or gold," and this pot was of iron.

Stella. Silly Bobbinette, if it had been glass it would have broken, and if gold, it would have melted and that would be worse luck. Come, put that old dream book away. What do you think papa will say when he sees me in this dress. Won't he be surprised and pleased. I look like a gypsy, don't I ?

Bobbi. [*Aside.*] I'm not so sure that the master will be pleased.

Stella. Ah, there he comes now ; just slip in here and' watch me surprise him. [*Ex.* **Bobbi.** *at* R. *Enter* L. **Rayburn** ; *walking with hesitation, as one blind.* **Stella** *dances softly before him.*]

Stella. Why, papa, you don't even seem to see me.

Ray. [*With a start.*] Ah, Stella, to be sure ; I am very absent-minded. Ha, ha, how dull I'm growing.

Stella. Well ?

Ray. Hey ? Well ? Oh yes, a kiss, I suppose ; there, you little tyrant.

Stella. Oh, daddykins, you are just too bad ; not a word about my pretty dress.

Ray. My delightful daughter, your old daddykins is an absent-minded old bear. To be sure, your dress. Very pretty indeed. Let me see, have I seen you wear it before? The fact is, a young lady's dress is something of an enigma to me.

Stella. Now papa. Of course you never saw it before, for I have only just found it in one of the old trunks which Bobbinette keeps in the west wing. She was airing some things, and I found it and these. [*Shakes castanets.*]

Ray. Stella, child, what mummery is this?

Stella. Why, daddy dear, I believe you are blind.

Ray. [*Aside.*] Blind! Ah, my God!

Stella. Don't you see, these go with the costume, the gypsy dress, for the dance, papa, that Bobbinette taught me. I thought you'd be pleased.

Ray. [*With agitation, feeling her dress.*] Take off the wretched trappings. Out of my sight with them. These garments of that accursed woman. [*Aside.*] Ah, what have I said, the mother of my Stella.

Stella. Oh, papa dearest, what have I done?

Ray. My darling, my little girl, forgive me.

Stella. You have spoiled all my pleasure, you naughty papa; and I wanted you to be pleased, too.

Ray. Forgive me, daughter, the sight of this dress [*sits with Stella on his knee*] has stirred some bitter memories. Is this—black lace?

Stella. Why papa, yes.

Ray. And these? [*Touching castanets.*] And what were you saying about a dance?

Stella. Oh, do you know I can do it better than Bobbinette now, papa, the peasants' dance, you know. Shall I show you? [*Dances a few measures, while Rayburn sits with head bent in gloomy reflection.*] But oh, daddy, you should have been there to have seen, and to have heard Andrew laugh at Bobbinette. Ah, but this is poetry, this is motion; it makes you glad to be alive. But you are sad to-day, papa. You are lonely. Why do we never go away from the island. Why do we not know people, other people besides Andrew and Bobinette and Dr. Fontaine?

Ray. Perhaps you may sooner than you think.

Stella. Oh, I think I should love to know another girl, papa. What a lot of things I should have to ask her. They must be very happy, the other girls.

Ray. Happy? What makes you think so?

Stella. Oh, because there are so many of them. Only think of having a new person to talk with every day. Of going to parties and balls ; Bobbinette has told me all about them. And I should have lovers, and sit in a box at the opera, with a pink satin cloak on. Oh, oh !

Ray. Lovers. Opera. Why you are only a baby yet.

Stella. But I shall be a woman some day.

Ray. Ah, too true ; but what if I tell you that you were soon to see New York—to go to school, to live there.

Stella. To *school.* Oh, you dearest daddykins. Really? When will we go ? Will Bobbinette go with us ? To New York. How delightful. [*Dances with joy.*]

Ray. But, my dear, *I* am not to be sent to school. *I* have no longing for the opera. Bird's Island is best suited to an old man like me.

Stella. Papa, what do you mean ?

Ray. Listen, my daughter, and I hope my Stella has too much good sense and reason to misunderstand me. Bird's Island is a very good place for a child, or for a gloomy old fellow like me, who likes a quiet life better than anything else. You have laid the foundation for a healthy, sound physique in the free unrestrained life you have lived here. But Stella, as you have just said, you will one day be a woman, and it is not fitting that the daughter of Alfred Rayburn should grow up, lacking accomplishments and polish, without which, native grace is at best rough and uncouth. You must be content, Stella, to leave me for a while. I have made arrangements to have you go to my old friend Richard Selwyn, for a short time at least. He has a daughter, and you will be with friends who will love you.

Stella. [*Throwing herself on her father's breast.*] Oh, how can you say so ?

Ray. For a short time, my love. [*Aside.*] Heaven forgive the deception.

Stella. I can never leave you. Are you sending me away —because—I—wanted to go ? Oh, papa, I will always be content to stay with you.

Ray. My daughter, my mind has been made up for some time ; it is best ; and Stella, you go to-day.

Stella. To-day, papa, how can you be so cruel.

Ray. Do you not think it hard for me ? Come, darling, don't make it any worse for us. Bobbinette knows, she is to go with you, so you will not be entirely with strangers. There, dry your tears, and let us go out on the beach and talk it over. Let us make this day as happy as we can. *Ex.* L. U. E. **Stella**

clinging to her father. Enter **Bobbinette** *with bandboxes and packages.*]

Bobbi. There, these are of the newest. I bade Andrew fetch me, from the town, two most suitable, and of the newest fashion ; one for the child, and one for me. One of dignity. Holy saints, but it is a long time since we had aught to do with fashions. Ah, but it is unchristian to live away from the world. I shall enjoy a little society myself. This Andrew, pouf, he is a stick, a clod ; he sees nothing. I shall see others who will have eyes, perhaps, for I dreamed a dream that betokens lovers also. [*Reads from dream book.*] " To dream of counting eggs, is a sign of lovers by the score." Ha, ha, and I was counting baskets and baskets of them. [*Laughs again, ; business with the boxes.*] Two bonnets of a shape the most fashionable, I told Andrew. Holy saints, I wonder which is for me, and which is for the child. 'Tis a shame to be so behind the style. [*Tries on first one then the other, looking in a hand glass for the effect.*] They are both strange. Surely this one suits my complexion best, but 'tis evident, a little gay. Perhaps it is this ; yes, most surely it is this ; I would not for any thing that we go to the house of Monsieur Selwyn with old fashions. No, we will hold our heads proud. Let it not be said that Bobbi-nette has no taste. There will be a butler, or some one, he, he. If he should think me striking—distingué ? Who could blame me if I make conquests ? Ah, I wish Andrew could be there to see. [*Ex. with affected airs,* L. I E. *Enter* **Stella** *and* **Ray-burn,** L. U. E.]

Stella. How lovely and blue the water is, daddy dear. Now that the time has really come, I feel as if it were wrong for me to leave you. You have only me. If my mother had lived— why, what is it, dear ?

Ray. Nothing, nothing, child ; don't mind me.

Stella. Of course, I was thoughtless to speak so abruptly of my dear mother. How you must have loved her ; I know you must, because you can never bear to speak of her ! but I wish you would, just this once. Was I a very little baby when she died ?

Ray. Yes, very little.

Stella. Poor, poor mamma ; and poor papa, to lose her. I wonder what it is like to have a mother ? Is Roberta Selwyn's mother living, papa ?

Ray. No, Mrs. Selwyn has been dead for several years. His sister-in-law is mistress of his house.

Stella. I feel so sad ; I think I am too young, daddy dear,

to have such an ache here. [*Lays her hand on her heart.*]
As you say, it is only for a little while.

Ray. My precious daughter. Would to heaven I could save
you every heart ache. But this separation is for your own sake.
Come love, cheer up ; look out over our island and let us remember our last day, for many days.

Stella. Oh, my father. I will be more courageons. It is
only for a little while, *isn't it?* Our lovely island, and our
dear bay, how I love them, now that I am to leave them. How
clear the water looks, papa.

Ray. With not a sail in sight.

Stella. Why yes, there are two.

Ray. Yes, yes, two, of course.

Stella. And on this side, see how the blue shows through
the delicate branches of the smoke trees.

Ray. Like glimpses of your blue eyes, my little girl.

Stella. [*Suddenly as the boat with* **Andrew** *comes in view.*]
Oh, the hateful sight.

Ray. What?

Stella. There, that.

Ray. But what?

Stella. Oh, papa, are you blind? Don't you see it is
Andrew with the boat that is to take me away from you. [*Enter*
Bobbinette, *with bags, boxes, wraps, etc.*]

Bobbi. Now, master, don't let the child be forgetful of her
new things. [*As* **Ray** *and* **Stella** *embrace.*] *Shouts to* **Andrew.**]
Andrew, are the boxes all safe? Is the boat dry, Andrew?
Come child. Ah master, have no fear, I will watch her as the
apple of your eye. Here Andrew, put these away safely.
[*Hands him parcels.*] Is the boat dry do you say? I would
not for anything soil our new apparel. Fear not master, the
child is safe with me. Bobbinette knows what is expected of
her, be careful of that box, Andrew.

Ray. Good-bye, darling, I will write you every day. [**Stella**
*starts toward the boat, runs back and embraces her father
again, is at last lifted by* **Rayburn** *into* **Bobbinette's** *arms.
The boat slowly moves out of sight. Tableau.* **Stella** *holding
her hands toward her father.* **Rayburn** *reaches out his in
answer, as the boat moves slowly off,* **Bobbinette** *waving her
handkerchief. Then* **Rayburn** *stands dejected with head bent
on his breast, with slow curtain. Music should accompany
the latter part of this scene.*]

ACT II.

[Scene :—*Home of* **Richard Selwyn** *in New York. A hand-somely furnished room.* **Selwyn** *and* **Mrs. McKillop** *discovered.*]

Sel. My dear Mrs. McKillop, I beg you not to trouble me with these trifles. Suppose the child is a little mischievous elf, she is only a child. For heaven's sake remember my digestion.

Mrs. McK. I should find it sair work to forget it, Richard Selwyn, with your constant complainin'. Mon, mon, why can't ye brace up a bit ? Ah, if I had ye up to Cairnavorgilly, the home of my ancestors, they'd teach ye to dance strathspeys and reels, and Gillie Callum, and toss the caber, and throw the hammer ; and eat haggis and drink whiskey and Athol brose, and——

Sel. Great heaven, spare me the history of your ancestry and their rude accomplishments.

Mrs. McK. Rude ? Rude ? Be ashamed to ye, Richard Selwyn. I'd have ye to know that I come from the Camerons of Aberlona. If ye ever knew anything, ye must know of York of M'Ouanall, who received thirty seven wounds, all mortal, at the battle of Inverlochy. It was a clan of unusual antiquity and power, and near cousin to the McFecknies of Gregarach.

Sel. Oh, this is worse than the rage about Stella. I tell you I don't care a straw about your Scotch genealogy. Go talk to Larry, he is Irish, and near enough of kin to be sympathetic.

Mrs. McK. Larry, gracious powers. Larry a neighbor and kinsman. An Irish bogtrotter. Ye insult the blood of all the M'Ouanalls, Richard Selwyn, when ye insult me. It's a bad sign, too, to be so quick to anger. A bad temper is a sad curse. The little savage that ye have been made guardian of is as like ye as your own.

Sel. Come, you have taken a dislike to the child because she plays pranks on you, isn't that the sum of her offences.

Mrs. McK. I hope I'm a Christian, and I take no dislike to any one. But this limb, this heathen, brought up without even a knowledge of the catechism, is a sore trial.

Sel. But what does she do ?

Mrs. McK. Do ? There isn't a mischief under the sun she

doesn't plan ; she hides my glasses—not that I wear them for
age, I'm near-sighted. She makes sport of my Gaelic songs ;
she makes me a laughin' stock. Oh, she's a limb.

Sel. You must try and make the best of her. My state of
health forbids excitement, as I told you more than once. I
esteem you, Mrs. McKillop, you keep my house admirably, but
I must be spared these little worries, and I insist—no more
biographies. [*Ex.* L.]

Mrs. McK. Ah, there is the makins of a man there. If I
but had him at Cairnavorgilly. [*Sighs.*] But he's deeficult,
he's deeficult. How my sister managed to catch him passes
me. [*Noise outside.*] Lord save us, here's that little savage
again. [*Enter* **Stella** *dragging* **Larry**, *entangled in a ham-
mock.*]

Stella. I've caught a fish, I've caught a fish. Oh, Mrs.
McKillop see him flounder. [*Romping with* L.]

Larry. Oh, for the love of heaven, miss, don't make a holy
show of me. Let me go now, that's a dear.

Stella. A talking fish, what a find. See him flop.

Mrs. McK. Ye disgraceful little heathen, ye limb of the
auld boy.

Larry. Oh, oh, ye mischief. There, I'm out. Ye monkey,
ye are as full of tricks as a sausage is full of mate. No ye don't.
[*Dodging her, runs off.* **Stella** *starts after him.*]

Mrs. McK. Will ye stop now ye little wild thing ? Don't
ye know better than to disgrace a dacint family rompin' with the
sarvints ?

Stella. Dear Mrs. McKillop, you called me a little savage
yourself, I'm only acting up to my character.

Mrs. McK. Ye needn't remain a savage, ye should take on
the ways of ceevilized people, when ye have the advantage of
associatin' with *me.*

Stella. Indeed ; but "it is deeficult, its deeficult." But do
you know Mrs. McKillop I have "done it" again ?

Mrs. McK. Maircy sakes, what have ye done ?

Stella. Oh, only one of the very many things I should not
do. There ought to be a printed book of the things one ought
not to do. It would be a large one.

Mrs. McK. Whatever do you mean, and what have ye done ?

Stella. Well you know Roberta took me to church with her,
I was never in a church before Mrs. McKillop.

Mrs. McK. Never ? Heaven presairve us.

Stella. No, there were none on Bird's Island you know. I
never supposed it would be wrong to sing at the church door.

Mrs. McK. Gude save us. What sang ye?

Stella. I only hummed a foolish little thing that I've heard Larry sing. [*Sings.*] Tarra-ra boom-de-ay.

Mrs. McK. Oh, ye little sauvage.

Stella. That wasn't all of my iniquity. I spoke out loud in church while we were waiting.

Mrs. McK. Maircy on us, what said ye?

Stella. Why, nothing, it was really such a little thing to make a fuss about. You see there was a picture of some sheep and a shepherd.

Mrs. McK. Yes, yes.

Stella. And I said suddenly, oh, Roberta, I think sheep look like people, don't you? Then she gripped me so tight by the arm, that I think it is bruised.

Mrs. McK. And no wonder,

Stella. But how stupid, to sit like that and never say a word. The preacher talked enough, when he got a chance.

Mrs. McK. Ye are hopeless I am afraid.

Stella. Yes, I am afraid so. But do forgive me Mrs. McGinty, this time.

Mrs. McK. McKillop, McKillop, ye daft bairn.

Stella. [*Affectionately disarranging* **Mrs. McK's.** *attire ; business.*] Dear Mrs. McKillop, do forgive me.

Mrs. McK. I doubt ye, I doubt ye.

Stella. Oh, no, you don't, you are a dear. And Mrs. McGinty—I mean McKillop—won't you please sing me one of your lovely Scotch songs?

Mrs. McK. For ye to make sport of? Not a bit of it.

Stella. Make sport of them, never. I want to learn some of them myself.

Mrs. McK. Eh? Maybe ye are showing signs of ceevilization, after all. I will then.

Stella. Wait a minute till I get the others to listen. [*Exit, returning immediately, pushing* **Selwyn** *and* **Roberta** *in front of her.*]

Mrs. McK. Ah, the dear child, she doesn't want to be selfish and enjoy all the pleasure herself.

Sel. There, there, my dear, excuse me this time ; I've heard Mrs. McKillop sing, and have no desire to repeat the experiment.

Stella. Yes, yes, do come in, and you, Roberta, sit there. Come in, Larry, I want you all. Now mind, everybody, *no conversation to disturb the musician.* Commence now, dear Mrs. McGinty—McKillop.

Mrs. McK. Ladies and gintlemen, ahem ; really these attentions flatter me. It's a good sign when ye manifest an interest in the poetry of auld Scotland and her songs. Ah, but I seem to see the clash of arms, the waving of banners, and the wailing of bag-pipes, when the mighty——

Stella. Yes, Yes, but the song, the song. [*A characteristic old song is sung, in a high-pitched old-fashioned tone during which they all leave one by one, except* **Stella.**]

Stella. Did he die ?

Mrs. McK. Did who die ?

Stella. The gentleman in the song.

Mrs. McK. There was nothing about death or a gentleman in the song. It was quite a funny little song of love, about a cow and a shepherd ; full of fun and merriment.

Stella. But surely someone groaned in the chorus !

Mrs. McK. Nothing of the kind ; that was probably an exclamation of joyful surprise.

Stella. What an expressive language.

Mrs. McK. Eh ? I doubt ye, I doubt ye. Eh, what ? [*To* **Larry,** *who enters and brings a card.*] Madame Helga. Ah, the child's governess and teacher. Show her in, Larry, and call Mr. Selwyn. Come child, with me, while the other people talk, and settle about ye. [*Ex.* L. *with* **Stella.** *Enter* **Selwyn** *and* **Madame Helga.**]

Sel. I am glad to see you, Madam Helga. I was about to go out for my morning walk—allow me to remove my wraps. These east winds play the mischief with me. I'm in very delicate health, very. What, with the east wind and the doctors, it's a wonder I'm alive. I have Dr. Smith for my chest, and he tells me my left lung is touched, and I must shield myself from the fog, *morning* fog especially. I have Dr. Jones for my liver, and he tells me I must walk constantly in the fresh air, *morning* air especially. So between them, I traverse the streets like a mummy. Thank heaven for a good constitution, my dear madam, for you see in me, a wreck—a wreck. [*Having removed wraps, sinks into a chair.*]

Madame Helga. I—am truly sorry, sir.

Sel. Oh, it's nothing new. People who see me every day, don't notice how ill I am. I'm so harrassed by conflicting opinions of doctors, that to have a fresh opinion like yours would be of value. Now, seriously, meeting me without prejuduce, would you say my liver was gone or not ?

Mme. Hel. [*Aside.*] What an extraordinary man. [*To* **Sel.**] Really sir, I am but little accustomed to illness of any kind ; but——

Sel. Madam, I ask you solemnly not to hesitate.

Mme. Hel. I do not think you look really ill.

Sel. [*With a sigh.*] Ah, I see how it is ; you are like all the rest, too kind to tell me what you see plainly in my face. Death, madam, death.

Mme. Hel. Oh, Mr. Selwyn, you frighten me. Is it so bad as that ?

Sel. Worse, much worse ; and I am a martyr to systems, erroneous systems past and present. My wretched digestion I inherit from men whose power were exhausted by our national kitchen. My present wretched condition has been achieved by the drugs in our national pharmacopia. I tell you, madam, a nation so behindhand in the first essential of civilization, the art of good cooking, is in the beginning of decay.

Mme. Hel. [*Aside.*] The man is surely deranged. May I ask, Mr. Selwyn, after my little charge ?

Sel. I beg your pardon for occupying your time, but you seemed so sympathetic. The little girl—yes, you will find her very bright, as girls go. Her father is a very peculiar man, secluding himself on account of family troubles, and bringing up his daughter on an island, you know. He changes his mind, however, and sends her to me, an old friend, to be educated. I advertise, you answer, and here you are.

Mme. Hel. Is your ward's mother dead ?

Sel. Ah, there is the sad part of my friend's story, She is not dead, but the child must remain in ignorance of this. She was an unworthy woman and broke my friend's heart. She made of the most genial man that ever lived, a gloomy misanthrope. But here are some other members of my family. [*Enter* **Roberta, Stella,** *and* **Mrs. McK.**] My daughter Roberta, my sister-in-law, Mrs. McKillop, and my ward, your pupil Stella.

Mme. Hel. Stella, I knew a little Stella once—a baby girl. What is your other name, dear.

Stella. Rayburn, madam.

Mme. Hel. Oh, my God. [*Starts.*]

Mrs. McK. Why, whatever ails the woman ? Here, stand back, loosen her neck, Roberta ; there, she's comin' out of it. I hope, ma'am, ye're not weakly ? Get away with ye, Selwyn, ye are a puir body at best. D'ye feel better, now ?

Mme. Hel. Thank you, no. It is nothing, I have been—not well.

Mrs. McK. Ye are not subject to such attacks ?

Mme. Hel. Oh, indeed, no.

Mrs. McK. It's well ye are not. Selwyn has a monopoly on 'he invalid business himself. My, but ye are a young woman, after all. How came ye with the white hair?

Mme. Hel. I am rarely ill; I will be better soon.

Mrs. McK. Well, ye don't look strong and hearty. Perhaps if ye are left a bit by yourself, it will do ye good. Get out, now, the lot of ye, and let the woman be quiet. Come, Stella.

Mme. Hel. Pray let the little girl remain, will you not?

Mrs. Mc.K. I'm afraid—varra weel then. Now mind, [*To* Stella] no pranks. [*Ex.*]

Mme. Hel. My dear, you are not afraid of me, are you?

Stella. Oh, no, only very sorry that you are ill.

Mme. Hel. What precious sympathy; and your name is Stella Rayburn? What is your father's name, dear child?

Stella. Papa's name is Alfred.

Mme. Hel. Ah, and your mother, little one?

Stella. My dear mother is dead, madam.

Mme. Hel. Dead! But of course you remember her death, perhaps?

Stella. Oh, no; I do not remember her, and my father can never bear to speak of her. He must have loved her very dearly, for it seems to hurt him so. My mother was very beautiful.

Mme. Hel. But how do you know?

Stella. I wear a locket with her picture. Look. [*Shows a locket from a chain at her neck.*]

Mme. Hel. [*Aside.*] My very self. [*To* Stella. And you wear this always?

Stella. Yes, always; I love to think that my beautiful mother is near me. Sometimes on the island, when the storm is loud, and I am afraid, I put my hand on my locket, and feel that I am not alone, and then I am not afraid any more.

Mme. Hel. Dearest child!

Stella. Bobbinette gave it to me a year ago, saying I was old enough to have it now, and that I must always wear it inside my dress, and not grieve papa by the sight of it.

Mme. Hel. Ah! Bobbinette was ever kind—that is—I mean is she quite well?

Stella. Yes, Bobbinette is never ill. She is here with me.

Mme. Hel. Here. [*Aside.*] Good heaven, she may recognize me.

Stella. I could never stay here without her. None of them love me, they all think I am strange and wild and ignorant. That funny Scotch woman calls me a little savage.

2

Mme. Hel. Unkind.

Stella. I dare say she doesn't mean to be unkind, and I play all sorts of pranks on her. And I am ignorant ; but you shall teach me to be——

Mme. Hel. More conventional, perhaps ; heaven forbid that you should be less natural. And you think we shall be good friends ?

Stella. I shall love you dearly if you will let me.

Mme. Hel. Let you. I am hungry for love, I have known so little.

Stella. Then I mustn't begin by tiring you. I'll run away now. When do we commence our lessons ?

Mme. Hel. Immediately.

Stella. I am so glad. I'll come again and show you the school room. Now just lie still and get well. [*Kisses her lightly on forehead, and ex.*]

Mme. Hel. [*Rising and pacing the floor.*] Oh, kind and gracious heaven, thou hast led me to this place. To see my child once again, my little baby girl, my Stella. I will teach her to love me. Ay, she loves me already. Then no one, not even her father, shall take her from me. But I must be on my guard. [*Looks in a mirror.*] Ah, no one can recognize me with this grey hair ; my face is pale too, white, washed out with years of weeping. But my child, I will have her again. I was weak and afraid in the old days, afraid of his terrible rage. But now, that I have seen her, have held her in my arms again, I will be strong, and no man shall take her from me. [*Ex. Enter* **Powers** *and* **Roberta.**]

Rob. I tell you we have not an idea in common. The old simile of the clinging vine, and the sturdy oak, is a back number. The American woman needs no oak, she looks for better things.

Pow. Er—yes ? Er—what, does she look for ?

Rob. For emancipation from the old bondage, social, political and civil.

Pow. Er—don't you think such violent change of base would result in social chaos ?

Rob. [*Grandly.*] Absolute justice has no need to concern itself with consequences.

Pow. You Americans are so—so intense. You take life so seriously.

Rob. I wish you would take me seriously now and then.

Pow. A—you know that I am ready to take you at any time. [**Roberta** *turns her back to him and looks out the window.*] I wish you would tell me—seriously, what you object to in my manner?

Rob. Oh you know well enough that you look with a sort of disdainful amusement on all the things that are of interest to me. You make fun of me when I express my sympathy with the aspirations of advanced womanhood. Oh yes you do, you know you do, you needn't deny it. Take only one thing for example; you have no sympathy, absolutely none, in one of the greatest efforts of the day; the effort of woman to throw off the shackles of conventional dress, when you know, you must know the disability it imposes.

Pow. Now really—er—you know the intricacies of feminine dress are an unspeakable mystery to me. The general effect is good. There are occult influences you know in a woman's dress which combine to give her the mysterious charm.

Rob. Oh, you talk like—a man. I wish you had to serve an apprenticeship, bound and hindered and hammered by these same "occult influences." How would you like to encase your waist in an unyielding armor? To repress and restrict your lungs to half their capacity?

Pow. Is it so bad as that? It must be then that an anatomical difference demands—er—that the female waist—receive more pressure than the male.

Rob. Oh you are *too* absurd, how can you be so frivolous about serious things?

Pow. I try to be—but you take up one so suddenly.

Rob. Oh, do I? Well you'll find I won't take you up so quickly as you seem to imagine. You Englishmen think all you have to do is to drop the handkerchief, and we American girls are ready to pick it up. I tell you I wouldn't marry you or any man, so there! [*Ex. and enter from the other side* Selwyn.]

Pow. How is a fellow to know? I haven't dropped any handkerchief.

Sel. Well, Powers, how goes your wooing with my daughter? I don't see why the deuce you young people can't get over this unholy habit of seeking to promote the general happiness of mankind by matrimony.

Pow. It *is* discouraging.

Sel. Then why do'nt you give it up?

Pow. But my dear sir, I'm in love with her.

Sel. Pooh. Tut. Young man, beware of all emotions, they are bad for the spleen. Love is an emotion. My daughter is a whimsical little wretch.

Pow. My Roberta, a wretch? She's an angel; her voice——

Sel. My dear fellow, don't roar like a bull of Bashan at m
I'm not in love, and I'm not deaf, and I *am* in delicate heal
Of course my daughter is all well enough, but I say she i:
whimsical little wretch—don't contradict me, the doctor has (
pressly forbid my being contradicted, I say she is whimsci
She has dipped into every new ism under the sun. First, i
Theosophy; then ethics ; then religion, why she changes h
religion with the season,.just now she is a socialist and reform(
Lord, Lord, the cranks and turns of the human mind. A f(
years ago socialism was banned ; now polite society flirts wi
it ; even the pulpit extends it the hand of fellowship.

Pow. All these are mere interests of the time.

Sel. You do'nt really want my daughter, my word for
you'd fight like cats and dogs.

Pow. [*Stiffly.*] I think you said you had no objection to n
marrying—Miss Roberta ?

Sel. Bless you, none in the world, if she will have you. B(
you would better take the advice of one who has tried matr
mony. Women are mostly cats. [*Ex.*]

Pow. Cats. What blasphemy. But he's my Roberta
father. She is an angel, a star. I suppose I'm pretty far gone
I did'nt think I could be so bad as this. [*Looks in a mirror,*]
do'nt seem the sort of fellow to tame a shrew, certainly. I'(
rather timid, and a trifle slow. I never could take a girl b
storm. Perhaps a long siege would do.

Bobbi. [*Enter reading aloud from a dream book.*] "T
dream of cutting ones nails of a Friday, without thinking of
raw cabbage, is a very good omen. It signifies wealth, posi
tion and a lover." Eh. This is Miss Roberta's lover. Is h
admiring himself, I wonder ? Par-don, but I expected to se(
Mr. Larry.

Pow. Mr. Larry, who is he ?

Bobbi. Oh but surely, he is the young man who make:
open the door.

Pow. Ah, I see ; yes-er and this Larry, is he attentive.

Bobbi. At-ten-tif ?

Pow. Is he courting ?

Bobbi. I think so.

Pow. You're not sure ? Do'nt you know when a man is in
earnest.

Bobbi. But surely ; yet this Larry is something slow.

Pow. How, I sympathize with him ; I'm something slow
myself. Tell me my dear-a-girl, I've a special reason for know-
ing ; how does a woman best like to be made love to ?

Bobbie. Do'nt you know ?

Pow. No ; I'm slow, like this Larry ; but you ought to have had lots of experiences.

Bobbi. Oh, yes.

Pow. Then tell me, do that's a good girl.

Bobbi. Well then-te-he ; a girl likes her lover not too shy.

Pow. Aha. Not too shy.

Bobbi. Not like a wooden man about the arms.

Pow. Not afraid to put his arm about her like this.

Bobbi. Yet not *too* bold.

Pow. Oh, certainly not.

Bobbi. Just bold enough ; even a chaste kiss is sometimes permitted.

Pow. Ha, ha ; something like this, eh ? [*Kisses her.*]

Bobbi. And if her head recline on his shoulder. [*Bus.*]

Pow. Yes, yes ; like this. Why you are an excellent teacher. Another kiss, Oh Lord ! [*Sees* **Larry,** *who has entered,*] Ha, ha.

Larry. Ha, ha.

Bobbi. Ha, ha.

Larry. [*Savagely.*] Ha, ha.

Pow. The fact is, Larry, she was teaching me——

Larry. So I see ; an' its an apt scholar ye are.

Pow. I hope so. In fact I should like to get on as fast as possible for I'm a novice myself.

Larry. Ye do well for a beginner sor.

Pow. Ha, yes ; I hope you do'nt mind. It was a sort of rehearsal you know. I'm much obliged to you ; and to you Bobbinette, and I think I shall get on pretty well now. [*Ex.* **Larry** *at opposite side of stage.*

Larry. I am sure he is welcome wid all me heart to his r-rehear-rsals.

Bobbi. [*Aside.*] He's jealous, and there's nothing like jealousy for bringing a man to his mind. I dream of anger last night, that's a sign of love.

Larry. But ye ought to time your r-r-ehearsals so that ye'll not be interrupted, so ye ought, Mistress Bobbinette.

Bobbi. Oh, Mr. Larry, you are not angry ?

Larry. Certainly not.

Bobbi. With Mr. Powers too.

Larry. I'm thinkin' Miss Bobby that ye are playing me for a sucker.

Bobbi. I know not that word, sucker.

Larry. Oh it's mighty innocent ye are ; have'nt ye been after recavin my attintions iver since ye came ?

Bobbi. Surely ; what then ?

Larry. Then why do I find ye with Miss Roberta's you
man's arm about ye, and, br-r-r-r. [*Starts to leave.*]

Bobbi. No do'nt go. It was all make believe.

Larry. Begorra, it looked like the rale thing.

Bobbi. But only to show him, he is timid, and Miss Robei
is strong, not clinging and and tender like me. [*Lays her he.*
on **Larry's** *shoulder.*]

Larry. Then let him practice wid Miss Roberta. I'll n
have any man practisin' wid the lady I'm r-rehearsin' wid m
silf. *Ex.*]

Bobbi. But this is too much impudence. Rehearsing wi
me ! Let see. [*Look through dream book.*] I dreamed of tl
east wind last night. East wind. "To dream of the ea
wind betokens a check to true love." Oh dear. Oh dear. [*E.*
Enter **Mrs. McKillop** *and* **Powers.**

Mrs. McK. You are varry right, Mr. Powers, I have recave
the greatest attention from gintlemen ; it has been the troubl
of my life to discourage the gintlemen.

Pow. But why discourage them ?

Mrs. McK. Hoots, mon ; ye would'nt have me marry ever
one of them and be a Mormon ?

Pow. Oh, I see ; but you were telling me about your lovers
Mrs. McKillop. Now, confidentially, how does a woman likt
best for a man to conduct his courtship ?

Mrs. McK. [*Aside.*] Gude lawk, does the man mean me
Ah, a man's heart must tell him that.

Pow. But you surely know what a woman prefers. Should
I, for instance, take her hand like this ? Should I be bold, or
timid ?

Mrs. McK. Oh be as bold as iver ye like, it becomes ye.

Pow. I will then, I will ; thank you dear Mrs. McKillop. I
will be bold and win her in spite of herself.

Mrs. McK. Eh ? Her ? Who ?

Pow. Roberta. Thank you ever so much. [*Ex.*]

Mrs. McK. The little beast. Well, thank heaven I did'nt
commit myself. *Ex.* L. *as* **Selwyn** *and* **Stella** *come on at* C.

Sel. But my dear little girl, will you be reasonable ? Your
father did not tell you of his threatened blindness, because he
could not bear to make you so unhappy, he knew you would
never have been willing to leave him.

Stella. That I would not, my darling papa.

Sel. He had no hope of recovery at first, but now he writes
me, that Sauvier, one of the most eminent oculists of Paris, tells

,im that there is every hope if he will submit to an operation.
;5o your father has conquered his aversion to meeting people,
ind is coming to New York for treatment.

Stella. He ought to have told me. Oh, my poor papa, to
;hink I have been so careless and happy, and my dear, dearest
,daddy blind. Oh, I can't bear it.

Sel. There, there, child, don't cry ; there is nothing worse
for the liver than grief. Besides, your papa is going to get well
.10w. [*Looks at letter.*] Why bless my soul, he may be here
it any moment. Dear me, I hope this excitement will not be
the end of me. [*Enter* **Larry** *at* c. *with* **Rayburn.**]

Larry. This way, sor, let me help ye, careful now, and may
the saints restore ye. Ah, here is the masther, and the little
leddy.

Stella. My father, my own daddykins.

Ray. My daughter, my little Stella.

Stella. Why did you send me away from you, my darling
papa, and you were blind ?

Ray. Do not speak of that now, we are together again, and
I am promised a hope of cure.

Sel. Rayburn, dear old fellow, haven't you a word for me ?

Ray. Selwyn. I never thought to meet you again, but fate
has ordered it otherwise. I could not keep my vow of seclusion, when there was a hope of seeing my child again. [*Kisses
her.*]

Sel. I deplore your misfortune, but I am glad it has broken
your resolve, for believe me, Alfred, the sacrifice was not
demanded.

Ray. Perhaps not. However, that is past, and hope once
more illumines my darkness. But how are you ? And how
much good it does me to hold your hand again, dear Richard.

Sel. [*Remembering his fancied illness.*] I am a wretched
hulk, a mere shadow of my former self, Bless my soul, I had
forgotten it for a few moments in the pleasure of seeing you
again. But I'm in a bad fix, Rayburn, a bad fix. [*Enter*
Madam Helga R.]

Mme. Hel. I beg pardon, I was looking for Miss Stella. I
was not aware, I will not intrude. Ah-h-h.

Ray. Who spoke ? What, I must be mad. Who spoke,
Selwyn ?

Stella. Come in, dear Madam Helga. Here is my father.

Sel. Yes, come in. This is your little pupil's father. Rayburn, this is Madam Helga, who has won all our hearts, your
daughter's first of all.

Ray. Madam, I am happy to meet you ; you see, I am blind.

Mme. Hel. [*Aside.*] Blind ? Heaven send me courage. Sir, [*to* **Ray,**] I am sorry for your misfortune.

Ray. Let me take your hand, madam ; you know we blind, read by touch, both books and people. Your voice moves me strangely, I have never met you, and yet—and yet—you are weeping, Madam Helga ?

Mme. Hel. It is for pity, sir.

Ray. Such sympathy is very sweet, I am sure you must be a good woman, and it is small wonder my daughter loves you. Your voice has a tone of sadness, and you are a young woman are you not ?

Mme. Hel. My hair is quite grey.

Stella. But I don't believe you are old, are you, dear madam.

Mme. Hel. From bitter sorrow, yes.

Ray. That voice ! My long seclusion has made me fanciful.

Stella. Oh, I am so sorry. Papa, may not Madam Helga belong to us now, and shall not we make her happy again ? When *you* are cured, and we are all happy once more ?

Ray. We will do what we can, my darling. Perhaps in lighting the gloom for others, my own way may be brightened. Let us hope, madam, that the future holds enough joy, to cancel the sorrow you have known.

Mme. Hel. Amen. And you, sir ?

Stella. Yes, and you, dearest daddykins, you shall see once more, and we'll never be sad again.

Ray. So be it. If heaven shall restore my sight, dear child, I will forget all the bitterness of my life, and remember only I have you.

Mme. Hel. Forget the bitterness ?

Ray. [*With a start.*] The bitterness ? Yes, I will forget.

CURTAIN.

ACT III.

[Scene :—*Same as Act II.* **Bobbinette** *and* **Larry** *enter.*]

Bobbi. I like not the new teacher, Mr. Larry. There is something—I know not what. But how she looks at my master, —and she with the gray hair,—the shame of it ?

Larry. But Bobby, me darlin', ye don't suppose the heart grows gray too ? Now, I'm no spring chicken, and ye know ye ain't so young yerself, as ye used to be.

Bobbi. Comparisons are always unpleasant. I like not that any strange woman should look with love at my master. And she cannot look at me. She avoids me.

Larry. Why what's to hinder his marry'n again ? Sure its a fine man he is, barrin' his blindness.

Bobbi. [*Mysteriously.*[Trouble will come of it. You do not know everything, Master Larry. Look here. [*Shows dream book.*] I dreamed of a yellow cat last night. " To dream of a yellow cat, is a great misfortune, a token of the greatest misfortune to your friends."

Larry. Ah, bother with yer dhrame book ; ye meant something else, now ye know ye did,

Bobbi. Never mind, I keep my master's secrets.

Larry. A woman kape a sacret, is it.

Bobbi. You shall see that I can. I will pray the saints for his safe delivery.

Larry. Arrah, now thin, I've heard of prayin' for strange things ; there are the faith cure paple, who pray the skins off ther petaties, and cure their childer's colic wid prayin', instead of peppermint. But I niver heard of prayin' to cure a man of matrimonial intintions, an' I don't belave ye can do it, Bobby darlin' if it once strikes in. [*Enter at* c. **Roberta** *and* **Powers.**]

Larry. [*Drawing* **Bobbinette** *to one side.*] Arrah, here come two that need prayin' for, for a quarer sparkin' I niver saw. Would ye observe thim now ?

Rob. I wonder if anything could shake your composure and calm self esteem. Could any thing shock you ? Or is that too violent an emotion for you ? I've a notion to try, at all events, for anything would be better than the evenness of your temper.

Pow. Do you want me to storm and swear at you.

Rob. It would be a variety, Listen. Beginning with to-morrow, I am going to adopt the reform dress ; there, what do you say to that ?

Pow. I—a—say that you are sure to grace any dress you may put on,

Rob. Nonsense, you only think of compliments. Do you know what it is ?

Pow. I'm not sure ; is it—are they—bloomers ?

Rob. It is a modification of that idea.

La:ry. Holy saints, its the breeches she manes. Let's be off, Miss Bobby, these young people talk about quare things. [*Ex.*]

Pow. Yes ? I have seen it—er—them. But to use your quaint southern vernacular, I thought it was—they were a " plum sight."

Rob. That is because your taste is perverted. Why should a woman be a slave to costume ?

Pow. Oh, really, I don't know, don't you know. But you see some of the women who wore this costume, were not—they were far from sylphlike ; to put it more plainly, they were quite the reverse.

Rob. Well, what of that ? All the more honor to their courage.

Pow. Yes, I admit it was an act of the highest heroism for a woman of 200 pounds to display her—her rotundity—if you please, in that dress. I am afraid the ovations she received were not calculated to make it a popular fashion.

Rob. Ovations ?

Pow. The people laughed, you know ; and the small boys,—well you know what the small boy is.

Rob. [*Fiercely.*] I should like to—*spank* the small boy.

Pow. Oh—certainly—ha—by all means. Ha, ha, I really thought you were about to commence with me.

Rob. Pooh, you are in no danger.

Pow. I wish you would let me tell you just how much danger I am in. Ah, will you, Roberta ?

Rob. What is the use ? You know we don't agree about anything, and you wont even take a decided stand, and quarrel about it. You know I don't care anything about what people call *love*. Bah, it makes me sick. I want a career. I want to work for the emancipation of my sisters ; I want to strike at the chains of woman's slavery. I want to help women up—up, into the arms of——

Pow. [*Eagerly.*] Yes, yes, so do I, I want to help one

voman up into the arms of—into my arms. [*Takes her in his rms.*]

Rob. *Mr. Powers.* You are too bold. [*Ex. with a sweep-ng courtesy.*]

Pow. There it is again, "*too bold.*" Now, how the deuce is . fellow to know how to be just bold enough? I consider that ather neat, you know, but she didn't seem to take it at all. 3ut, by Jove, what eyes. They are a full furnished battery ; .nd when she turns them on me, I feel a shower of bombs and .ll manner of combustibles and explosives thrown right into the :entre of my dazzled sense. At all events I must keep it up ;)erhaps Bobbinette would give me another lesson. [*Ex. Enter* **Rayburn,** *groping his way and stumbling.*]

Ray. I must give up trying to find my way about alone. 3ut I have hated to be led by any other than my little Stella. \h, God, if this should be a hopeless experiment, I could not)ear it. I wonder where all the chairs have hidden themselves ; \nd who is it that says the devil is always in inanimate things ? *Enter* **Madame Helga,** *who stops at* c. *door.*]

Mme. Hel. [*Softly.*] Alfred.

Ray. Who speaks ?

Mme. Hel. [*With an effort at control.*] You are alone, Mr. Rayburn, shall I help you to a chair? It is I, Madame Helga, your daughter's governess, you know. Sir, you are trembling. [*He sits.*]

Ray. Ah, yes ; Madame Helga. Why is it your voice always startles me ?

Mme. Hel. I am sorry sir if my voice disturbs you.

Ray. It is a beautiful voice ; it is so like, and so unlike. [*To himself.*] It is strange, her voice had not the ring of sad-ness. You have known great sorrow, I am sure, madame ?

Mme. Hel. Bitter sorrow.

Ray. It is the common lot. It is a mocking fate that pro-mises so much, and gives so little.

Mme. Hel. But you, surely your worst grief is about to be dispelled ? When you shall have recovered your eyesight——

Ray. Yes, yes, I should have nothing to regret then. Will you sit down with me, dear madame. My little girl loves you so dearly, that I am drawn toward you myself. Perhaps it is the common bond of grief. Tell me of yourself ; believe me I do not ask through idle curiosity, but I wish to be your friend.

Mme. Hel. I thank you. The friend who should be nearest and dearest, owes me justice, rather than friendship. But I ac-cept your friendship and sympathy.

Ray. That is well, give me your hand on it. [*Takes her hand.*] This hand is soft and small, yet there is strength in it It seems the hand of a woman not old. I thought you said youı hair was gray, madam ?

Mme. Hel. It is gray, but not altogether with years.

Ray. [*Kissing her hand.*] It is sad that a woman, a tendeı woman should suffer. Have you lost your loved ones ?

Mme. Hel. Yes.

Ray. By—by death ?

Mme. Hel. Alas, no ; through the demon of anger, hastε and injustice.

Ray. But may not all be well again ?

Mme. Hel. If my husband abates one jot of his self love, sir, which has blinded him to the truth, and ruined his life and mine, perhaps I may hold my child in my arnıs and call heı mine before the world. [*He grows agitated.*] But I am wrong to agitate you with the recital of my grief ; forgive me. I know that the success of the operation on your eyes depends on your tranquility.

Ray. Nay, it is only pity, believe me. [*Enter* Stella.]

Stella. Dearest papa, I've been up to your rooms looking for you. Did you find your way alone. Why did you not call me ? I'm my papa's eyes now, Madam Helga ; and I've finished my exercises too.

Ray. What a diligent child. Is she a dreadful ignoramus, madam ?

Mme. Hel. She is very bright, and will learn rapidly.

Ray. I have taught her only in a desultory sort of way ; she knows nothing of text books.

Mme. Hel. So much the better.

Ray. [*Rising.*] Ah, you agree with me that oral teachinȝ is best. Is it not time for our walk on the verandah, my child ?

Stella. I am all ready.

Ray. Will you go with us, madam ?

Mme. Hel. Thank you, no ; I have other duties.

Stella. Come then my big boy, my darling child, that I have to take such good care of—put this scarf about your neck ; here is your hat, now hold tight to my hand. [*Ex. through* c. *door.*]

Mme. Hel.]*Looking after them. Enter* **Bobbinette** *at* L.] Ah, my starved heart. My husband—my baby girl.

Bobbi. Aha, what did I say ? Oh, that yellow cat, that yellow cat. I beg pardon, madame——

Mme. Hel. Ah, it is you ?

Bobbi. Yes, it is I. You appear to be interested, madame.

Mme. Hel. Oh, yes, in my pupil. [*Aside.*] Can it be that he suspects me ?

Bobbi. And in her pupil's father, is there any faith to be put in dreams. Have you seen Miss Roberta ? I have a note for her from Mr. Powers.

Mme. Hel. I think she is in the library.

Bobbi. [*Seeming to wish to draw* Madam Helga *into conversation.*] Ah, there be a beautiful couple soon, when Miss Roberta gets tired playing fickle.

Mme. Hel. Love is a beautiful thing.

Bobbi. It is. [*Aside.*] The maneuvering wretch. [*Aloud.*] dreamed of scratching Miss Roberta's nose, last night with a thistle.

Mme. Hel. [*Smiling.*] Yes ?

Bobbi. That means a kiss from a beard.

Mme. Hel. That will be her father, perhaps.

Bobbi. Not a bit of it ; there's not a word in my dream book about fathers. And look, I dreamed that master caught a fox with a red tail, and that is a sign he will never marry. [*Ex. spitefully.*]

Mme. Hel. Bobbinette distrusts me, but does not recognize me. If I could only trust her. [*Ex. after* Bobbinette. *Playing of bag-pipes outside, and enter* Mrs. McKillop *and* Selwyn.]

Sel. I have told you over and over, Mrs. Killop, that I must not be excited.

Mrs. McK. Now what is more soothin' to the narves than music ? Just tell me, Richard Selwyn, are ye tired of me in his house ?

Sel. No, but tired to death of your importunities, your Gaelic song and that villainous boy you insist on having to play that devilish instrument. For heaven's sake go out and send him away. Here, [*Goes to door,*] if you don't take that thing away, I'll come out and send for the police. [*Voice outside, All right, sir."*] When you know that my life depends on my being kept from annoyance. If the rinderpest had broken out among all the cats of Scotland, Mrs. McKillop, it couldn't be worse ; but I draw the line at bag-pipes.

Mrs. McK. Ah, weel, I'll send him away since ye've no music nor poetry in yer sowl ; I only live to please you, Richard. [*With a languishing look.*]

Sel. [*With some alarm.*] Yes, yes, that's all right. I don't want to be hard on you, but my nerves you know, my nerves.

Mrs. McK. All your imagination, why I have no nerves.

Sel. I can well believe it.

Mrs. McK. All of my family, except your wife, my sister Morna, were robust and strong. At eighty-nine, my grandmother, Mrs. McKechnie, of Jilly-wheezle, had a cheek like an apple.

Sel. Hum, yes, apples. Apples always give me an infernal indigestion.

Mrs. McK. Now if ye were to marry again, Richard.

Sel. Marry. Why great heaven, woman, I'm a physical wreck.

Mrs. McK. But if ye married some strong body, not *too* young and feckless.

Sel. [*Excitedly.*] Never, never, Mrs. McKillop, are you proposing to me ? Never I tell you. [*Enter* **Stella.**]

Mrs. McK. What do ye mean, child, by intrudin' ? Ye were listenin' ye little sauvage.

Stella. I would not be so mean ; you know I was not. Were you saying hateful things of me, that you think so ?

Mrs. McK. I belave ye lie, ye little mousin' thing, ye. It's no more than might be expected of your mother's child. Oh, you needn't turn on me, Richard Selwyn, you that puts me like dirt under your foot and this sly child of a dissolute woman to come up and spy on me.

Sel. Woman, be silent.

Stella. I have learned many things in a few months. I never dreamed a woman could be so cruel and mean as I know you to be ; ignorant, cowardly and untruthful. I should hate you if it were worth while.

Mrs. McK. What, what, ye daur, ye daur——

Sel. Come, come ; let this stop. Stella, go away and forget what she has said.

Stella. It is fitting that such a woman as you should traduce my beautiful dead mother.

Mrs. McK. Beautiful ! Dead ! She's no more dead than I am, but livin' in eeniquity in some foreign town I've no doot.

Sel. Hold your tongue, you old Jezebel ; Stella, leave the room, the room, the woman is insane.

Mrs. McK. Woman, no more *woman* than you are yourself, Richard Selwyn. [*To* **Stella.**] If ye don't belave it, ask your father. [*Ex.*]

Stella. Oh, Mr. Selwyn, I feel so strange. How could she say it ! You don't look at me, Mr. Selwyn. What did she mean ? I'll ask my father.

Sel. No, no, child I forbid you.

Stella. You forbid me? You are not my father, I will obey him. [*Turns to leave.*]

Sel. Would you kill your father with excitement, or run the risk of exciting him so that the operation will be impossible?

Stell. My poor father, my dear father. Oh, Mr. Selwyn, there seemed to be truth, yet no, how could it be true? Mr. Selwyn, I am older than I look, tell me, relieve this dreadful suspicion; tell what she meant. She said, *my mother was living*, not dead. And you looked so strange at her yourself, Oh, Mr. Selwyn, tell me.

Sel. I could cheerfully hang that old harridan. Well then, Stella, since so much has been told you, since you have a suspicion of the truth, it is as well to tell you the whole. Your mother, my child, is not really dead, but separated from your father. But do not, as you value your father's peace of mind, and his life, really, let him know that you have grown old enough. Come, child, don't get so white.

Stella. *My mother living.* But not, not, wicked as she said? Say no, Mr. Selwyn. Oh, I know it is not true, but even if it were, my mother, my mother!

Sel. There, there child, how can I know? I dare say she was good. Your father separated himself from her and took you away with him; none of his friends ever knew the cause.

Stella. Oh-h, how unhappy this world is; God is very cruel.

Sel. My little girl, you are much too young to have known this. Now don't take it too much to heart. You do not remember her, so she can be nothing more than a sentiment to you. Go and amuse yourself, and try to keep up your spirits for your father's sake. I could murder that old catamaran. I suppose I shall pay for this with a relapse. Here is a book of drawings, now do try to forget all about it. And be a happy child again. [*Ex.*]

Stella. [*Letting the book of drawings slip from her lap.*] Forget all about it, be a happy child again. Oh–h–h, I feel like an old, old woman must feel. " I do not remember her, so she can be nothing but a sentiment to me." Nothing to me? I've thought of my mother, dreamed of her every night since I can remember. Often at night, on Bird's Island, when the storm rocked the house, and I was *so* afraid, for *I was such a little thing to have no mother*, I have thought of her, and prayed to my mother in heaven; and now, Oh, I can't bear it, I can't bear it. Mother-mother! [*Throws herself sobbing on the floor.*] [*Enter Madame Helga.*]

Mme. Hel. I thought I heard some one weeping. Why
Stella, my child, my darling. Ah do not weep, my own, be
comforted. But what is it?

Stella. Oh, it is nothing ; that is——

Mme. Hel. Ah the pity of it. The pity of grief for one so
young ; my child will you not tell me, who loves you?

Stella. My heart is broken.

Mme. Hel. Nay, nay, dear one, sorrow lies not so heavily
on youth, believe me.

Stella. But Oh I hate her, how I hate that horrid old woman.
I should like to kill her.

Mme. Hel. Ah, God, the passion ; how like the father. Try,
try always my own, pray that you subdue the swift unreasoning
temper. It is that which has ruined my life.

Stella. I think I must tell you, you are good and kind, anc
I cannot endure it alone. She said, Mrs. McKillop said, that
my mother whose very name I have worshipped, was, not dead
but living, and a wicked woman. Oh Madame.

Mme. Hel. [*Springing to her feet.*] Tis false. Ah, pitying
heaven what am I to do? It is not true, loved one, believe he-
not. Your mother was never wicked, never bad ; mistaken
perhaps, and not brave enough, but always true. Ah, God
what am I saying?

Stella. [*Clinging to her.*] But, Madame Helga, how can
you know? Can have known her?

Mme. Hel. Sit down child, I have alarmed you. [*Sits near*
Stella, *and holds* **Stella's** *hands clasped to her breast.*] You
love me, do not you?

Stella. Oh, yes, dear Madame.

Mme. Hel. If I answer your question will you be content to
wait, to know no more at present, but trust me until I am able
to tell you that which shall change your life, perhaps make it
happier?

Stella Yes, I think so ; there is no one to comfort me, but
you.

Mme. Hel. Dear one ; then listen. I knew your mother
she was not the wicked woman they thought her. She never
deceived your father intentionally, but foolishly and through
ignorance, and then in fear. In his terrible anger he would
hear no explanations, but with many bitter words took you away
and left her alone. [*Weeps.*] Your mother has suffered bitterly,
but she lives, truly, and in good time you shall know her.
When she is ready to lay before your father the proofs of her
innocence——

Stella. [*Interrupting springs to her feet, and gazes into* **Mme. Helga's** *face. She snatches the locket from her breast and compares the pictured face with the face before her, then falls at her knees.*] My mother, my mother! Oh there is no need to wait, you are my mother! I know, I know! If my father were here! Oh, I shall die with joy.

Mme. Hel. But child, Stella, you do not know——

Stella. Do not deny yourself to me, my mother, put your arms about me and say I am indeed your child, as I know I am.

Mme. Hel. My love, my baby girl! It is heaven's will. God has given you to me sooner even than I would.

Stella. And to think I was so unhappy. Oh, I will never be sad again, I will even forgive Mrs. McKillop, for she never knew you.

Mme. That is right, my darling. Do not harbor the black shadow of hatred in your heart. Let us go some where to enjoy our love where we will not be disturbed.

Stella. My darling mother. [*They start out but are arrested by seeing* **Powers** *and* **Roberta** *enter, assisting* **Rayburn.**]

Ray. You are very kind, my dear; Every one makes me feel my old self again. [*They seat him at* L.]

Roberta. And now dear Mr. Rayburn, promise us, that when you have once regained your sight, that you will never seclude yourself from your friends again.

Stella. [*Coming across.*] Dearest father, was not your heart always warmed with my love?

Pow. Excuse me—er—dear young lady. "Dearest father" is hardly correct form. That would imply that you had more than one father, eh?

Ray. And one poor old blind daddykins is enough? [*Caresses her.*]

Roberta. We were looking for you Madame Helga, to beg you to give us some music.

Ray. Let me add my entreaties also.

Mme. Hel. I am very glad if I can please you. [*Goes to piano at* R.]

SELECTION.

Pow. Ah, that was rather sad, you know. Could'nt you play us something brighter, Madame? *She plays the Spanish dance, the air that affected Ray. in Act* I.]

Ray. [*Starting up wildly.*] No, no, not that. That maddening air is burned into my very brain. Every chord and

2

measure stirs the gall and bitterness of my soul, and I curse
again the woman whose falseness makes it a hateful memory.
I live again the misery of the past——

Stella. My—father—no, no.

Ray. My daughter. Friends, forgive me. Madame Helga,
forgive a man, old before his time, shattered and broken by
illness and sorrow, and *blind*, Madame Helga, remember that,
I beg of you to play what you will—the melody you have begun,
I insist in it. I am better now. [RAY *near the piano.* **Madame
Helga** *plays Spanish dance softly.* **Stella** *kneels at her
father's side looking at him, his head sunk on his breast as if
in reverie.* **Roberta** *and* **Powers** *at opposite side of stage.
They look at each other,* **Roberta** *gives him her hand, which
he kisses. An effective second curtain discloses* **Rayburn**
*alone on the stage as in reverie, while at the back, as in a
picture, a Spanish dancer dances to the air played softly by
the orchestra.*]

CURTAIN.

ACT IV.

[**Scene** :—*Interior at Bird's Island.*]

Mrs. McKillop. There is some mystery in the house. Ever
since we came to Bird's Island, because Alfred Raymond was
determined to look for the first time on his island home, there
has been such a whispering and sly slippin' aboot. And the
little sauvage is as sweet as honey to me, an' bears me no ill
will for me unfortunate burst of temper. Ah, the McFecknees
ever had the hot blood. It leps along me veins as did
McOuhannal's of old. Even Raymond is kind and gracious to
me, though he must know of the disclosure I made. Perhaps
he means—Lawk, who knows? He, he, I'd be a stepmother
to the little sauvage. I shall keep my eyes open, I'm not to be
kept in the dark alone ; the curiosity of me sex must be satis-
fied. [*Ex. Enter* **Richard Selwyn.**]

Sel. This climate is paradise itself. I have scarcely thought
of my heart since we came. And now, if our double experiment is only successful, the experiment on his eyes, and the one

on his heart. To-day the bandages are to be removed, and if all goes well he will see once more. Then we will bring about the reconciliation with his wife, who is an angel ; yes, an angel, even I must admit that, though I still contend that angels are not frequent. But the evidence in favor of her innocence and purity is undeniable, Rayburn must see it. Besides, he is already as dependent on her as if he knew her to be his wife. Ha, ha, I feel something of the same delight that a matchmaker must feel, in bringing these two together. Well, it is a new sensation at all events to forget myself. [*Enter* **Roberta** *with downcast head and lagging step.*] Oh, Roberta, is there anything the matter ?

Rob. No, papa.

Sel. But you look tired.

Rob. We have been walking over the island, and fishing on the coast.

Sel. We ?

Rob. Mr. Powers and I.

Sel. Oh, oh ; and that is why you are tired ? Didn't Powers help you over the cliffs and stones ?

Rob. Oh, yes ; he carried the basket—and rod.

Sel. Was that all ?

Rob. Well, you see papa, there was nothing else to carry except *me*, and I suppose that didn't occur to him.

Sel. What do you mean by hiding your face in this way? Look at me Roberta. Let me see your tongue. Clean, all clean. Your pulse then. [*Feels her pulse.*] Too quick, too quick ; I must have Smith write you a prescription. Come into the library with me till I give you a dose of calomel.

Rob. I—don't think I need calomel, papa. [*Hangs her head.*]

Sel. Eh ? What's this ? You're not in love, Roberta ?

Rob. [*Indignantly.*] Of course not, papa.

Sel. Dear, dear, I never would have believed it of you, Roberta.

Rob. You know that I think there is nothing so ridiculous, so vulgar, as falling in love. But, [*sadly*] one has human sympathies—and I feel sorry for him.

Sel. I understand, you are going to take him to get rid of him ?

Rob. Oh no, indeed ; if it—were—not for the sound of his voice, papa, and his eyes, and—oh, papa. [*Hides her face on his shoulder.*]

Sel. My dear daughter ! There, mind my left lung. God

bless you my dear. But it is a risk. Lord what a risk. [*Enter* **Powers.**] Well, sir, I suppose you come to ask my consent ?

Rob. Oh, no, no, indeed, papa ; he has not—oh indeed you are mistaken.

Pow. Eh? Er—consent.

Sel. Why God bless my soul, man, don't you want to marry my daughter ?

Rob. Oh, papa, how can you ? You were entirely mistaken. I never said that this is—Mr. Powers has not—oh, what have you done ? [*Starts to run.*]

Pow. [*Intercepting her, and taking her hand.*] Ah—don't go yet ; that is, I hope you won't go. A—let your father decide for us.

Rob. There is nothing to decide. Let me go—please let me go.

Pow. Beg pardon—just one minute you know ; there is, something to decide.

Sel. Why, what is all this about.

Rob. Nothing at all papa ; please let me go.

Pow. Er—won't you wait one moment, please ? Mr. Selwyn, don't you think Roberta ought to marry me ?

Rob. Absurd ; how should papa know ?

Sel. This is a singular courtship, upon my word. Do you love my daughter, sir ?

Pow. [*Quickly.*] Oh, yes, yes ; [*to* **Roberta**] you know I do.

Sel. And Roberta, do you love him ?

Rob. [*Impatiently.*] How can I tell ? You ought to know, papa.

Sel. Oh, well, if you leave it to me, I pronounce it a case. [*Spreads hands over them in mockery.*] Bless you my children. And now, you'll excuse me from staying to witness the spooning. Lord. [*Aside.*] Roberta spooning must be a sight for the gods to weep at. Besides, like Solomon, I'm sick of love. [*Ex.* **Powers** *and* **Roberta** *remain standing, holding each other's hands ; they burst out laughing.*]

Rob. An excellent joke. Ha, ha.

Pow. Capital. But—we're engaged, you know ?

Rob. Oh, I suppose so.

Pow. And you're in love with me, too ; your father says so ?

Rob. Yes, papa says so.

Pow. Oh, Roberta.

Rob. Oh, Arthur.

Pow. Who would have supposed she wanted it done in this

way ? A—Roberta, does your heart beat like ten thousand trip hammers ?

Rob. Yes, Arthur ; and I hear something like electric bells ringing in my ears.

Pow. Then your father was right, it *is* a case. Ah—love is a very peculiar thing, don't you think ? Now, do you know, when you look at me like that with your lovely eyes, I feel as if the ground was swept from under my feet, and I stood on rosy clouds of bliss.

Rob. It is a rather interesting experiment. I never supposed there was so much science in it.

Pow. Oh, Roberta.

Rob. Oh, Arthur. But must I give up all my hopes of—of —reform and—everything ?

Pow. Certainly not ; only—er—limit your field of work to— to—well, say to me. [**Larry** *and* **Bobbinette** *cross at back of stage.*] There are another pair of lovers ; let us go out on the beach before they see us.

Rob. Oh, yes, I'm ashamed of it too.

Pow. Eh, what ? Do you think I am ashamed of it ? I'd put my arm about you like this, [*Bus*] and kiss you like this, and this, before the whole world.

Rob. Oh, would you, really ? Why, Arthur, I never dreamed you had so much decision. [*Ex.* **Bobbinette** *and* **Larry** *come on.*]

Bobbi. This is the great day, Mr. Larry, which shall determine whether our master shall ever see again. I dreamed three times last night of an eagle flying against the wind ; but there is not one word in my book about eagles. I am all impatience till the bandages are removed. After ten days the good doctor said. Was it not like master to bring us all back to the Island ? He wanted to look first on his dear home, he said.

Larry. ' Dear home,' indade thin, I tell ye flat, mistress Bobbinette if ye kape praisin' this lonesome place, ye'll disgust me, that's what ye will. An' if ye can't lave it wid a better grace, we can never make a match of it. This buryin' ground is no place for a fine young man like mesilf ; no Broadway, no thayatres, no nothing.

Bobbi. Young man, hum'ph, master impudence.

Larry. But I dare say nayther of us will regret it ; ye will always have the remimbrance of the chances you *have* had. As for me—

Bobbi. As for you ?

Larry. Oh, I can amuse myself, disportin' down the streets, and schmilin' at all the pretty girls that wink at me.

Bobbi. I am sure its nothing to me how the pretty girls wink. If they knew the perfidy of men—as I do, they would wink—*never*.

Larry. Oh, thin, let us drop the subject by all manes. Good morning, mistress Bobbinette. [*Ex.*]

Bobbi. But what? He's gone. There is nothing like this in my dream book. Men are deceitful ever. Ah me, I am much troubled. With this Larry so—so indifferent, and this woman, this Madame Helga, so quiet, so evidently *determine* to marry my master. What then? She already winds him around her finger—so. He calls never for Bobbinette ; but always for *"Madame Helga."* Even all the others she have bewitch. Mr. Selwyn thinks no more of his liver, his lights, his heart, or his insides any where, but he too is charmed to wait on *"Madame Helga."* [*Enter* **Madame Helga.**]

Mme. Hel. Were you talking to yourself, Bobbinette.

Bobbi. Perhaps, when one is distracted with trouble and annoyance, one does not know.

Mme. Hel. Poor Bobbinette, have you troubles too?

Bobbi. But yes ; what then? I can be nothing to *Madame Helga.* She is become the favorite of every one. She is so—so—what shall I say? She lead every one by the nose.

Mme. Hel. That was spitefully said. Tell me, Bobbinette, why of all in this house will you be the only one who hates me? Why should you hate one who does you only kindness?

Bobbi. I am not so sure of that. [*Turning swiftly on* **Madame Helga.**] It is this, madame, though it ill becomes me to speak so bold. You are trying to win my master's heart.

Mme. Hel. And what then?

Bobbi. Eh? What then? She owns it.

Mme. Hel. It is true I possess Mr. Rayburn's confidence, and Stella's love, are you jealous of that?

Bobbi. Nothing but unhappiness can come of it. Can you keep a secret? Master already has a living wife. What, that does not move you?

Mme. Hel. Did you know her?

Bobbi. Know her? Ah, mon dieu, but yes. The sweetest lady that ever smiled, Some cruel mistake it must have been that parted them, for master loved her dearly.

Mme. Hel. You are faithful to her memory, Bobbinette?

Bobbi. But yes, and shall be always,

Mme. Hel. Would you know her now, think you, Bobbinette? It is a long time since you saw her?

Bobbi. But I should know her.

Mme. Hel. And would you help restore her to her husband's love?

Bobbi. Ah, surely.

Mme. Hel. Time and tears will have changed her, Bobbinette.

Bobbi. But not to my eyes; I should know her among a thousand.

Mme. Hel. [*Tearing off her glasses.*] Bobbinette.

Bobbi. But what? What trickery is this? My mistress, my loved and honored mistress! [*Falls at* **Madame Helga's** *feet and kisses her hands and dress.*] Oh, the dear hand, thin with grief, and oh, the grey hair. Sorrow, sorrow. What must you have suffered, my dear, dear mistress.

Mme. Hel. My faithful Bobbinette. I should have known that I might trust you; [*kisses her cheek*] but I was afraid. You will keep my secret yet a little while longer?

Bobbi. Do you doubt me? How blind I have been, my sweet mistress. And you—and master—you will be happy again?

Mme. Hel. I hope for that. Sh—here he comes. [*Enter* **Ray** *and* **Stella.**]

Ray. Do not be too hopeful my darling, if it should prove not successful.

Stella. But it will, it will; I'm sure of that. God will answer our prayers. Oh, here is my—Madame Helga and Bobbinette.

Ray. I knew you must be somewhere near, madame, I think I must feel your presence. I seem to be unusually sensitive to-day. And you, my good Bobbinette, have I your prayers too? Surely all must go well.

Bobbi. Oh, master, master. [**Madame Helga** *holds up a hand warningly.*]

Ray. Come, no tears to-day, unless joyful ones. Sit near me, Madame Helga. On this day, when every one seems full of a suppressed excitement, strange to say, I feel a curious calm. It is as though my spirit, so long tossed about by the storm of despair, would never know unrest again. [*During this time* **Stella** *and* **Bobbinette,** *have in pantomime shown a knowledge of the secret. They embrace and presently slip out leaving* **Madame Helga** *and* **Raymond** *alone.*]

Mme. Hel. Heaven grant that it may be so.

Ray. Amen.

Mme. Hel. Every soul believes it's own shadows the darkest.

Ray. Ah, true. I had forgotten your shadow, your sorrow ; hope and happiness have made me selfish. Why not tell me of yourself now, dear madame ? You say your husband is still living ?

Mme. Hel. Yes.

Ray. [*With a sigh.*] And you love him still ?

Mme. Hel. I love and honor him above all men, and ever have.

Ray. Then why——

Mme. Hel. Not to-day, dear Mr. Rayburn ; my story is too stormy, and you must be kept quiet, must be calm to-day.

Ray. But somehow I feel to insist. Tell me of yourself— now. Have I not deserved your confidence ?

Mme. Hel. You have. [*After a pause.*] It was a cruel mistake parted us. Listen. I was an opera singer and dancer, poor and humble, when my husband met me and took me out of a life that was most distasteful, and made me his loved wife. We were not acquainted long before our marriage, and he supposed I had no family. I was ashamed to tell him of my only brother, who had been committed to prison for some youthful folly. He was never bad, but weak, and his wild associates led him astray. He made his escape, and came to me, and threw himself at my feet, begged me to protect him. 'Twas there my husband found him, and went into one of those dreadful rages that always frightened me dumb. He was beside himself with passion, and I was beside myself with terror. I could not speak. He cursed me in wild rage, and took our child and went away. Ah, I cannot speak of that day. I was so young, so ignorant ; I dared not ask after him ; I was never brave. So my brother and I went and hid ourselves in Paris for awhile, and then to the little village where we were born ; and I sewed and taught music, and kept us until my brother died.

Ray. And you never sought out your husband to tell him of his cruel blunder ? Why this is incredible ; any man in his senses would have listened.

Mme. Hel. True, but he was not in his senses. He was raving. And I was so ignorant and afraid.

Ray. But good heavens, this must be righted.

Mme. Hel. [*Laying her hand on his arm.*] Do not agitate yourself on my account. Some day he will let me atone.

Ray. Let you atone ? Why he must be a monster of in-

credulity to doubt you. What atonement does he not owe you?
[*Sinks into a reverie ; gradually a suspicion dawns on him.*]
God ! How like ! What if there should have been a doubt?
[*A glimmer of the truth comes to him.*] Let me hold your
hands in mine a moment, Madame Helga. They tremble.

Mme. Hel. With emotion at your sympathy. Pray sit
down, Mr. Rayburn, remember you promised me I should not
excite you. Think, the doctor will be here very soon now. I
will never forgive myself. Do sit down.

Ray. [*Firmly.*] There is a ring in your voice, that I heard
when I first met you. You have striven to conceal it since.

Mme. Hel. Oh, no, no. [*Aside.*] What can I say?

Ray. Say, say if indeed you are Bertha. Say if you are in
truth my wronged and suffering wife. I WILL SEE. [*Tears off
the bandage.* **Madame Helga** *shrieks, and all come on the
stage.*] It is my wife. God forgive me. [*Faints ; they lay
him on couch.*]

Mme. Hel. Alfred, husband, speak to me. [*To* **Selwyn.**]
Oh, say I have not killed him.

Sel. I think not. There, he's coming out all right. Rayburn, old fellow, how do you find yourself?

Ray. I see ! I see ! Oh, the blessed light that showed me
my wife's face—her dear face. Where is she? [**Madame
Helga** *kneels at his side.*] This dear, true face. God's own
light on the face that ever looked truth back again. Blind?
Aye, I was blind then when I doubted you. The brief darkness
I have known since, was nothing to my wilful blindness. Not
at my feet, dear one, to my heart, to my heart. [*Rising.*]

Stella. Oh, I shall die of happiness.

Ray. My little girl, do you see your mother?

Stella. Oh, I have known her all along.

Ray. Ah, yes, only I have been blind.

Sel. We have all been in the conspiracy, Rayburn.

Ray. Let me look at you, dear friend. If happiness could
kill—My wife. I can never restore these gray hairs, but I can
reverence and worship them. [*Kisses her hair.*] And atone
by my devotion for every day and hour.

Mme. Hel. I think our little Stella was keener of sight than
anyone.

Stella. Why of course, any girl would know her ownest—
mother. My father and mother, what a happy girl I am. Is it
not a beautiful world, Roberta?

Ray. [*With uplifted head.*] A beautiful happy world, my
wife, where God's sunlight drives away every shadow.

Stella. [*Kissing* **Mrs. McKillop.**] And ought not everybody love *everybody.*

Rob. *and* **Pow.** [*At* L. 2 E.] So they ought.

Larry *and* **Bobbinette.** [*At* R. 2 E.] So they ought. [**Selwyn** *and* **Mrs. McKillop** *at back ; they look at each other,* **Selwyn** *turns away his head.* **Rayburn** *and* **Madame Helga** *at* C. *while* **Stella** *dances softly in front of them. Music of a Spanish dance.* ·

CURTAIN.

www.ingramcontent.com/pod-product-compliance
Lightning Source LLC
Chambersburg PA
CBHW061237260626
47172CB00003B/899